Dear Parent:
Your child's love of reading starts here!

Every child learns to read in a different way and at his or her own speed. Some go back and forth between reading levels and read favorite books again and again. Others read through each level in order. You can help your young reader improve and become more confident by encouraging his or her own interests and abilities. From books your child reads with you to the first books he or she reads alone, there are I Can Read Books for every stage of reading:

SHARED READING
Basic language, word repetition, and whimsical illustrations, ideal for sharing with your emergent reader

BEGINNING READING
Short sentences, familiar words, and simple concepts for children eager to read on their own

READING WITH HELP
Engaging stories, longer sentences, and language play for developing readers

READING ALONE
Complex plots, challenging vocabulary, and high-interest topics for the independent reader

ADVANCED READING
Short paragraphs, chapters, and exciting themes for the perfect bridge to chapter books

I Can Read Books have introduced children to the joy of reading since 1957. Featuring award-winning authors and illustrators and a fabulous cast of beloved characters, I Can Read Books set the standard for beginning readers.

A lifetime of discovery begins with the magical words "I Can Read!"

Visit www.icanread.com for information on enriching your child's reading experience.

Pinkalicious®

School Rules!

To Zelda, Grace, and David
—V.K.

The author gratefully acknowledges
the artistic and editorial contributions
of Daniel Griffo and Susan Hill.

I Can Read Book® is a trademark of HarperCollins Publishers.

Pinkalicious: School Rules!
Copyright © 2010 by Victoria Kann

PINKALICIOUS and all related logos and characters
are trademarks of Victoria Kann. Used with permission.

Based on the HarperCollins book *Pinkalicious* written by
Victoria Kann and Elizabeth Kann, illustrated by Victoria Kann

Library of Congress catalog card number: 2009053452
ISBN 978-0-06-192886-4 (trade bdg.) —ISBN 978-0-06-192885-7 (pbk.)

18 19 20 SCP 10 9 8 7
❖
First Edition

I Can Read!

BEGINNING READING 1

Pinkalicious®
School Rules!

by Victoria Kann

HARPER
An Imprint of HarperCollinsPublishers

School is okay.

Except for one thing.

When I am at school,

I miss Goldilicious.

Goldie, for short.

Goldie is my unicorn.

I really like my teacher.

His name is Mr. Pushkin.

I have some friends in my class
and I made a new friend yesterday.
But I miss Goldie anyway.

This morning when I woke up

I had a very good idea.

I could bring Goldie to school with me!

School would be
perfectly pinkatastic
with Goldilicious
there, too.

There was a shiny red apple
on Mr. Pushkin's desk.

Goldie took the apple
and nibbled it gently.

Mr. Pushkin heard Goldie munching
and he thought it was me.
"Pinkalicious, there is no eating
until snack time," he said.
"It's the rule."

"It's not me," I said.

"It's Goldilicious, my unicorn!

She didn't eat much for breakfast,"

I added.

Mr. Pushkin smiled.

He took me aside

and he told me that unicorns

are not allowed in school.

"It's the rule," he said.

Rules are something

I do not love about school.

And I really do not love

the rule about no unicorns.

I began to cry a little.

I cried a little harder.

"Okay, Pinkalicious,"

said Mr. Pushkin.

"Your unicorn may stay,

just this once."

I stopped crying.

In fact, I clapped and twirled.

"But if your unicorn stays, you must teach her the rules," Mr. Pushkin said. "Do you think you can do that?"

"Yes!" I said.

"I know I can!"

At reading time,

Goldilicious was very quiet.

Goldilicious helped me with my math.

Unicorns are very good at counting.

When it was time for recess,

I showed Goldilicious

how to line up by the door.
Goldilicious did not push

or wiggle or cut the line at all.

Goldilicious played nicely

with the other kids.

Everyone had so much fun
with Goldie and me.

I didn't know I had

so many friends at school!

Soon it was time to go home.

Goldie got my backpack
off its hook.

"Tell me, Pinkalicious,"

said Mr. Pushkin.

"Did you and your unicorn

have a good day?"

"We sure did!" I said.

31

"School rules!"